TONY BRADMAN MARTIN CHATTERTON

The Surprise
PARTY

For Lily and Oscar
T.B.

To everyone at Shoreside School
M.C.

First published in Great Britain 2004
by Egmont Books Ltd
239 Kensington High Street, London W8 6SA
Text copyright © Tony Bradman 2004
Illustrations copyright © Martin Chatterton 2004
The author and illustrator have asserted their moral rights.
Paperback ISBN 1 4052 0756 6
10 9 8 7 6 5 4
A CIP catalogue record for this title is available from the British Library.
Printed in Singapore.

Contents

Red Bananas

A Special Day

It was Sunday afternoon in the Land of Sand, and in the pyramid where the Mummy family lived, things were . . . well, pretty much the same as usual.

Daddy Mummy was asleep in front of the TV. The Mummy kids, Tut and Sis, were doing some painting and making a terrible mess. And Mummy Mummy had just come back from the Memphis Mall.

'Did you have a good shopping trip, dear?' said Daddy Mummy, once Mummy Mummy had managed to wake him.

'Not bad,' said Mummy Mummy. 'There's a terrific sale on at Isis Stores. I got us some new bandages, some new sheets for our coffins . . . oh, and I bought a nice card for Grand-mummy Mummy and Grand-daddy Mummy.'

'A card?' said Daddy Mummy. 'But why do we need a card for them?'

'Don't you remember?' said Mummy Mummy, giving him one of her cross looks. 'It's their wedding anniversary next weekend. On Saturday, they will have been married for, let me think . . . yes, exactly five thousand years.'

'*Five thousand years!*' yelled Daddy Mummy. 'Why, that means . . .'

'They're even older than we thought,' said Tut.

'They can't be,' said Sis. 'Nobody's *that* old.'

'No, no,' said Daddy Mummy, jumping up, 'it means it's a very special day, so we ought to do something very, er . . . *special* for them. After all, you don't celebrate that kind of anniversary every day of the week, do you?'

'That's true, I suppose,' said Mummy Mummy. 'Although if ours came round more often even you might remember it.

What do you have in mind?'

'Umm . . . we should definitely have a party,' said Daddy Mummy.

'Hey, outstanding idea, Pop!' said Tut.

'This mummy is a genius!' said Sis.

'And we should invite everybody we know,' said Daddy Mummy.

'They'll have the time of their lives!'

'We'll hire somewhere to hold it,' Daddy Mummy went on, 'and a band to get everybody dancing, and have a huge cake, and . . . I'll make a speech! And how about this, kids – we could make it a surprise party! We'll keep it a secret from Grand-mummy Mummy and Grand-daddy Mummy until the very last minute! Won't that be great?'

'Hurray, a surprise party!' Tut and Sis yelled, leaping up and down.

'Well, dear, what do *you* think?' said Daddy Mummy eventually.

Mummy Mummy was standing there looking grim, her arms folded.

'I think it could go horribly wrong,' she said. 'Besides, it's an awful lot to get organised in less than a week, and I'm certainly not doing everything.'

'But of course not!' said Daddy Mummy, beaming. 'That wouldn't be fair. I'll do my share, I promise! In fact, we *all* will, won't we, kids?'

Just leave it to us!

Tut and Sis stopped leaping up and down, and started nodding instead.

'Somehow that doesn't make me feel any better,' Mummy Mummy muttered. Then she sighed. 'Oh well, you win. Grand-mummy Mummy and Grand-daddy Mummy deserve a treat.'

Almost Bursting

A little while later, the Mummies were getting ready to have tea when there was a loud knocking on the front door – Knock Knock! Knock Knock!

'Yoo-hoo!' said somebody outside. 'It's only us!'

13

'Oh no!' said Daddy Mummy. 'It's Grand-mummy Mummy and Grand-daddy Mummy! Right, kids, remember – not a word about the party, OK?'

'Our lips are sealed,' said Tut.

'We'll see,' said Mummy Mummy. 'I'll give you five minutes before you both start blabbing.'

Daddy Mummy frowned, and the Mummy kids glared at her. But Mummy Mummy ignored them, and went to open the front door.

'Hi, everybody!' said Grand-daddy Mummy. 'We were just passing, so we thought we'd drop in. Hope you don't mind – we won't stay long.'

'And how are our favourite grandchildren today?' said Grand-mummy Mummy. 'Any chance of a couple of kisses for your favourite old granny?'

'Sure,' said Tut. 'But you *are* pretty old, aren't you?'

'Yes, you must be more than five . . .' Sis began to say.

'OK, who'd like a nice cup of tea?' said Mummy Mummy quickly. It was her turn to glare now, and Daddy Mummy did some of his own glaring too.

But it was no use. Tut and Sis were almost bursting to tell the secret. No matter what Mummy Mummy and Daddy Mummy did, the Mummy kids kept dragging the conversation back to Saturday and parties.

Grand-mummy Mummy and Grand-daddy Mummy were soon looking puzzled, and finally Mummy Mummy could stand it no more. She flashed Daddy Mummy a You-Deal-With-Them glare and took Grand-mummy Mummy upstairs.

'So then, you two,' said Grand-daddy Mummy after they'd gone. He put his tea cup down on the table, tapped his ear and shook his head a couple of times. 'Er . . . tell me, have you been doing anything exciting recently?'

Tut and Sis looked at each other, then at him. '*Only planning a surprise party for your five-thousandth wedding anniversary!*' they said together in a rush.

'I'm sorry, kids, what did you say?' muttered Grand-daddy Mummy, tapping his ear again. 'My blasted hearing aid's been playing up again . . .'

Daddy Mummy grabbed Tut and Sis and hurried them out of the room.

'Back in a minute, Grand-daddy Mummy!' he yelled over his shoulder.

'You two should be ashamed of yourselves,' said Daddy Mummy. 'Off to your tombs, the pair of you, and take those blasted paint sets with you as well!'

'Huh, that's blown it,' Tut muttered as he and Sis trudged through the pyramid. 'I bet they keep us out of everything now.'

'So what?' said Sis. 'We could always do something for the party ourselves . . . and keep it a secret from *them*.'

'I like it,' said Tut. 'But what shall we do? We need a good idea.'

Upstairs, Mummy Mummy had been showing Grand-mummy Mummy the new sheets. Tut and Sis looked at them . . . and at their paint sets.

And then they turned to each other, and smiled . . .

So Much to Do

At breakfast the next day, Mummy Mummy and Daddy Mummy put together a list of the things that had to be organised for the party.

'See, there's so much to do!' said Mummy Mummy, looking depressed.

A mummy's work is never done!

'Don't worry, dear,'
said Daddy Mummy. 'I'll
book the venue. What do
you think of the Great
Pyramid? It's the only
place that's big enough.'

'It will be expensive, too,'
said Mummy Mummy. 'And
what about the band? And
the food and drink? We'll
need to find good caterers.'

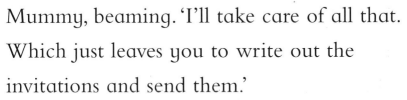

'No problem,' said Daddy
Mummy, beaming. 'I'll take care of all that.
Which just leaves you to write out the
invitations and send them.'

'I can do that,' said Mummy Mummy.
'I'll start this morning, although perhaps
I ought to go shopping first. I'll definitely
need a new outfit.'

'And I'll make a few phone calls,' said
Daddy Mummy. 'Although I might work
on my speech first. I'll need to get that right,
won't I?'

'Bandages . . . hat . . . shoes . . .' Mummy
Mummy was murmuring. 'Hey, where are
the kids? Hurry up, you two! You'll be late
for school!'

Tut and Sis were busy doing something in their room.

'Sorry, Mummy Mummy!' yelled Tut. 'Just coming!'

'We'd better make sure it's hidden,' Sis whispered.

'They won't find it under here,' Tut whispered back.

'See you later, dear,' Mummy Mummy said
to Daddy Mummy, and they left.

'What? Oh, right,' said Daddy Mummy.
He was scribbling away on a piece of
papyrus. Then he frowned and screwed it
up. 'Yes, see you later . . .'

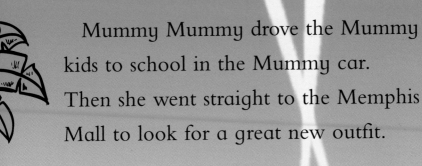

Mummy Mummy drove the Mummy
kids to school in the Mummy car.
Then she went straight to the Memphis
Mall to look for a great new outfit.

Daddy Mummy kept working at his speech all that day . . .

and all day Tuesday . . .

Mummy Mummy went shopping, and tried on lots of different outfits.

And as for the Mummy kids — well, Tut and Sis managed to keep themselves pretty busy, too. Secretly busy . . .

Then on Friday, Mummy Mummy decided to do some checking up.

'You *have* remembered to book everything, haven't you, dear?' she said.

'What?' said Daddy Mummy, screwing up the piece of papyrus in front of him. 'Of course I have! Er . . . excuse me, I just need to make a phone call . . .'

'He *must* have booked the Great Pyramid,' Mummy Mummy muttered. 'But I bet he's forgotten the band and the caterers. I'd better book them both myself!'

Mummy Mummy logged on to the MummyNet, and started searching.

Meanwhile, Daddy Mummy was hurriedly scanning the small ads in the *Memphis Times*, and trying to remember what he had, and hadn't done.

And the Mummy kids were feeling very pleased with themselves . . .

Surprises All Round

Early on Saturday, Mummy Mummy called Grand-mummy Mummy and Grand-daddy Mummy, and arranged to meet them at the Great Pyramid.

Then the Mummy family got ready, and set off in the Mummy car. They parked, and went straight up to the elegant mummy at the reception desk.

'Hi there,' she said. 'How may I help you? A booking for a party, you say. Well, I'm afraid we don't seem to have anything in your name . . .'

'Oh, no!' groaned Daddy Mummy. 'I must have forgotten to do it . . .'

Typical!

'Huh, I knew this would happen,' Mummy Mummy muttered. 'Oh, well. Do you have a room we could book? We'll need something pretty big.'

'Alas, we're full,' said the receptionist. 'As you can see, we're hosting the annual conference of the SSS – the Society of Sarcophagus Salesmen . . .'

'What now?' said Daddy Mummy. 'The guests will start arriving soon!'

'Ah . . . I don't think they will,' said Mummy Mummy, suddenly looking rather uncomfortable. 'I, er . . . forgot to write the invitations and send them.'

'I don't believe it!' laughed Tut. 'What a dozy pair!'

What are you two like?

'You got that right,' said Sis. 'Hang on, who's this?'

'*Ola, amigos*!' shouted a mummy who had just come in. Behind him stood a crowd of mummies wearing large hats and carrying guitars. 'We are the Mambo Mummies, and we are here to play at the anniversary party!'

'Hey, that's a coincidence,' said another mummy. He and the three mummies with him were wearing sharp suits, and carrying guitars and a drum kit. 'We're the Scarabs, and that's what we're here for too . . .'

It seemed that Mummy Mummy and Daddy Mummy had each booked a band. They had also each booked different caterers, so it wasn't long before the main entrance to the Great Pyramid was very, very crowded.

'This is a disaster!' said Daddy Mummy. 'I think we should go home!'

And so they did. They sneaked out without anyone noticing. But there was more to come. In fact, there were surprises all round.

Mummy Mummy called Grand-mummy Mummy and Grand-daddy Mummy, and told them not to go to the Great Pyramid. She invited them round instead. When they arrived, Mummy Mummy gave them the card she'd bought . . . and Daddy Mummy made his speech.

'Here goes,' he said shyly. 'Ahem . . . er . . . congratulations!'

Everyone waited for more, but Daddy Mummy just beamed.

'Is that it?' said Tut. 'He's been scribbling for days!'

'It's all we need to hear,' said Grand-mummy Mummy. 'Isn't it, dear?'

Eh? Speak up, woman!

'Sorry, what did you say, dear?' said Grand-daddy Mummy. 'Oh yes, quite right. Actually, we're relieved you didn't go to a lot of trouble. We were worried you might, and we certainly wouldn't have wanted that.'

'Really?' said Mummy Mummy. 'Er . . . good job we didn't, then.'

TA-DA!

HAPPY A
GRAND-MUMMY MUMMY

'Still, I wish we'd done *something* special,'
said Daddy Mummy.

'Well, we have!' said Sis. 'Come on, Tut,
let's show them . . .'

Tut and Sis unrolled a huge banner. They'd
tied the new sheets together with bandages.

I don't
believe it!

What does
it say, dear?

Surprise!

NIVERSARY
GRAND-DADDY MUMMY!

Grand-mummy Mummy and
Grand-daddy Mummy were delighted,
of course, and hugged the Mummy kids.
Mummy Mummy and Daddy Mummy
stood there looking stunned for a moment . . .
but they ended up smiling too.

I knew they
were up to
something!

What a
wonderful
surprise!

'Everything seems to have turned out fine, dear,' said Daddy Mummy.

'Now there's a surprise,' said Mummy Mummy. 'OK . . . *let's party!*'

And then the whole Mummy family had a very good time indeed.